For David, Melody, and Daye
– Lisa Wilke Pope

To Clayton County, Iowa
– Arthur Geisert

All of the illustrations in this book were produced from copperplate etchings
that were first hand printed and then hand colored using watercolor.

www.enchantedlion.com

First Edition published in 2021 by Enchanted Lion Books
248 Creamer Street, Studio 4, Brooklyn, New York 11231
Text copyright © 2019 by Lisa Wilke Pope
Illustrations copyright © 2019 by Arthur Geisert
Production and layout: Lawrence Kim
All rights reserved under International and Pan-American Copyright Conventions
A CIP record is on file with the Library of Congress
ISBN: 978-1-59270-314-2

Printed in China by RR Donnelley Asia Printing Solutions Ltd.
First Printing

How the Big Bad Wolf Got His Comeuppance

Lisa Wilke Pope   Arthur Geisert

BIG LOAD WASHERS

Enchanted Lion Books
NEW YORK

When the Big Bad Wolf got hungry,
he had a reputation for huffing and puffing
and blowing houses down
in order to eat their inhabitants.

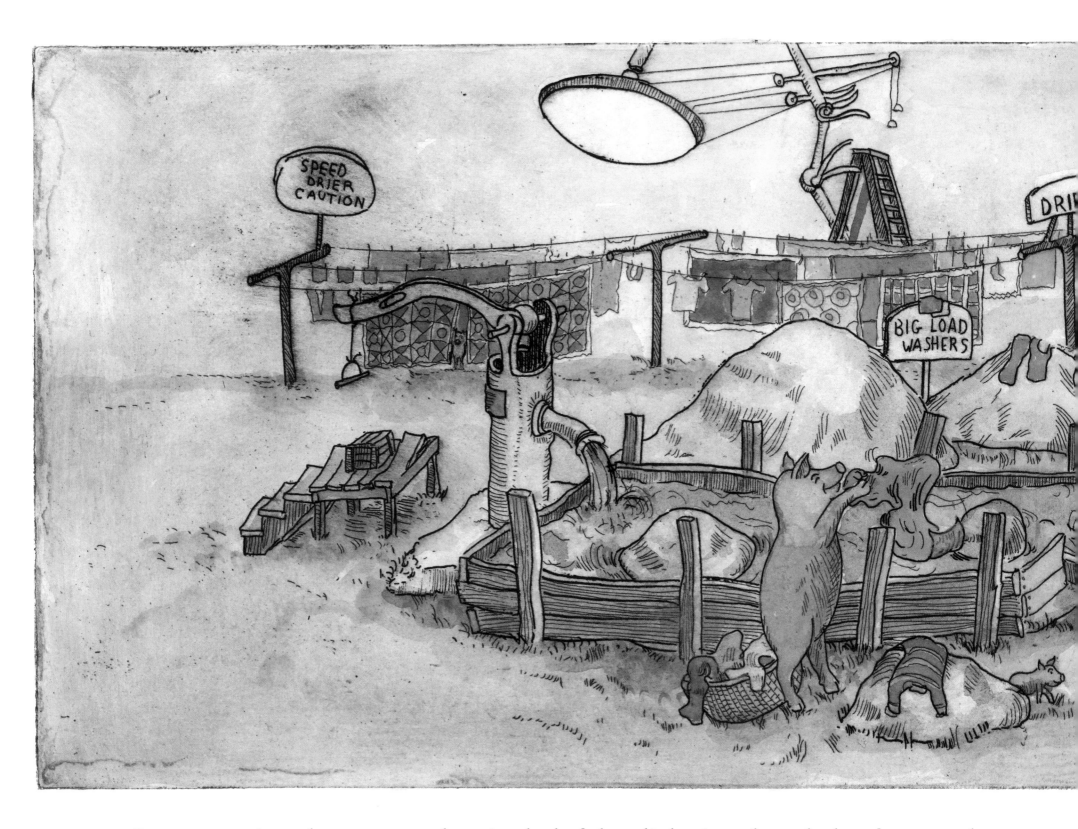

Once upon a time, there was a mother pig who had three little pigs, whom she loved very much.

Even though she worked hard every day, she struggled to make ends meet.

After a particularly miserable dinner, she explained that the time had come
for them to go out into the world to seek their fortunes.

She warned her little pigs to be wary of the wolf and sent them off early the next morning.

Eventually, the wolf came upon the first little pig, who had found a harvested field
and made a house out of bundles of grass.

The wolf grew hungry.

What the wolf didn't know was that the little pig, heeding his mother's warning,
had built an elaborate underground contraption.

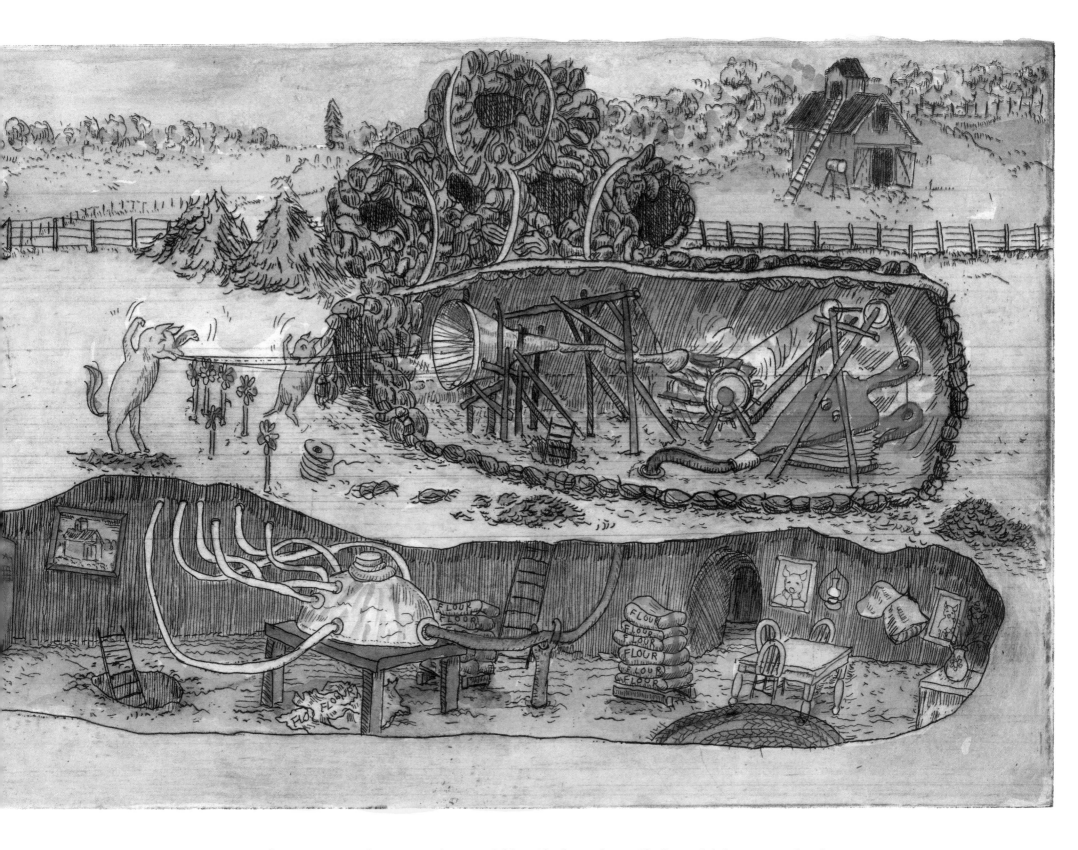

Determined to get at the pig, the wolf huffed and puffed and blew mightily,
in order to blow the house down.

To the wolf's great surprise, flour exploded from the flowers, blanketing him in fine, white powder.

Unbeknownst to the wolf, the clever little pig had engineered it to happen just that way.

Humiliated and still covered in flour, the Big Bad Wolf continued on through the fields until he saw a town.

The wolf was even hungrier than before when he came upon the second little pig among a large pile of construction materials.

The little pig intended to build a handsome home with a grand dome, but the wolf had other plans.

Full of confidence, the wolf huffed and puffed and blew mightily, in order to scatter the pieces far and wide.

To the wolf's great surprise, the pieces flew into the air, then fell into place, forming an impressive house. Unbeknownst to the wolf, the clever little pig had engineered it to happen just that way.

The wolf was infuriated that the little pig was out of reach but had no choice but to move on.

Twice foiled, the dejected wolf traipsed on until he came upon the third little pig,
who lived in a stately castle.

Famished and desperate, the Big Bad Wolf huffed and puffed and blew mightily,
in order to unleash a powerful blast.

To the wolf's great surprise, there was suddenly a deafening noise. The surge of air from the wolf's tremendous blast had set off an intricate alarm system of horns and whistles.

Unbeknownst to the wolf, the clever little pig had engineered it to happen just that way.
Covering his ears, the wolf ran away in defeat.

Back in his lair, the wolf searched his cupboards for something to eat but found nothing.

To take his mind off his growling stomach, the Big Bad Wolf took a boiling hot bath and lay down for a nap.

Soon, he was asleep and dreaming of a delectable pork dinner.